16

49p.

Tips for Reading Together

Children learn best when reading is fun.

- Talk about the title and the pictures on the cover.
- Discuss what you think the story might be about.
- Read the story together, inviting your child to read with you.
- Give lots of praise as your child reads with you, and help them when necessary.
- Try different ways of helping if they get stuck on a word. For example: read the first sound or syllable of the word, read the whole sentence, or refer to the picture. Focus on the meaning.
- Have fun finding the hidden reptiles.
- Re-read the story later, encouraging your child to read as much of it as they can.

Children enjoy re-reading stories and this helps to build their confidence.

Have fun!

Find the 10 different reptiles hidden in the pictures.

Dragon Danger

Cynthia Rider • Alex Brychta

OXFORD

UNIVERSITY PRESS

Floppy was dreaming about
dragons.

Floppy saw a baby dragon with
its mother.

The mother dragon saw Floppy.

"Go away," she roared.

The dragon roared again and
flapped her wings.

She flew towards Floppy.

"Oh help!" he said.

WHOOSH! Flames came out
of the dragon's mouth.

Floppy hid, but the
dragon saw him.

Floppy ran onto a bridge.
WHOOSH! More flames
came out of the dragon's mouth.

WHOOSH!!

"Help!" said Floppy.

"The bridge is on fire."

Floppy ran back across the
bridge.

He ran past a rock and saw the
baby dragon again.

The mother dragon roared at
Floppy. She flew up onto a
high rock.

Oh no! The rock started to fall.

CRASH! The rock fell
down . . .

but Floppy pulled the baby
dragon out of danger.

"Phew! Just in time," he said.

What a brave dog!

Think about the story

Why did the mother dragon roar at Floppy?

Why couldn't Floppy hide from the dragon?

How do you think Floppy felt when the rock started to fall?

What other dragon stories do you know?

now
know

A Maze

Help Floppy find his way out of the dragon's maze.

Useful common words repeated in this story and other books in the series.

again   but   came   of   onto   out   said   saw   she   the

Names in this story: Floppy

More books for you to enjoy

Level 1: Getting Ready

Level 2: Starting to Read

Level 3: Becoming a Reader

Level 4: Building Confidence

Level 5: Reading with Confidence

OXFORD
UNIVERSITY PRESS

Great Clarendon Street,
Oxford OX2 6DP

Text © Cynthia Rider 2006
Illustrations © Alex Brychta 2006

First published 2006

Series Editors: Kate Ruttle,
Annemarie Young

British Library Cataloguing
in Publication Data available

ISBN–13: 978-019-279233-4

10 9 8 7 6 5 4 3 2 1

Printed in China by Imago